Little Grey Rabbit

THE SQUIRREL, THE HARE AND THE LITTLE GREY RABBIT

Little Grey Rabbit

THE SQUIRREL, THE HARE
AND THE LITTLE GREY RABBIT

By Alison Uttley
Pictures by Margaret Tempest

templar
books

Along time ago, on the edge of a wood, there lived a hare, a squirrel and a little grey rabbit. The hare and the squirrel were very vain, but the little rabbit wasn't at all.

She would spring out of bed each morning and hurry around doing all the chores.

When the house was clean and the food was cooked she called, "Breakfast is ready!"

The others strolled downstairs.
"Lettuce again?" they said. "Can't we have something else?"

"The milk hasn't come yet," said Rabbit.

Just then a 'tap, tap, tap' sounded on the door and Hedgehog came in with a pint of milk.

"Watch out," he said. "A weasel has come to our wood." And off he hobbled.

Then another 'tap, tap, tap' came on the door. This time it was Robin Redbreast with the letters. He'd heard all about the weasel, too.

When Little Grey Rabbit went out, her
heart pitter-pattered, but she did not see the
weasel. She picked a prickly teasel brush
for Squirrel, then went to the Farmer's
vegetable patch to get carrots for Hare.

"You little rascal," shouted the Farmer when he saw her. "Just you wait!" But Little Grey Rabbit did not wait. She ran for her life – she hurt her paw, but still she ran.

"I won't go there again," she said to Hare and Squirrel that night. "I will ask Wise Owl how to grow our own carrots."

Later, Little Grey Rabbit crept outside to visit Owl.

"Wise Owl," she called up to him. "Will you tell me how to grow carrots?"

"Only if you give me your tail," said the Owl.

Wise Owl swooped down for her tail, then fastened it to his door as a knocker.

"You can grow carrots with seeds from the shop in the village," said Owl, and he flew away.

As Little Grey Rabbit walked back
through the woods, she came across the
weasel sniffing at her footprints. Very
quietly, she tiptoed out of sight, then
ran away home and crawled into bed.

The next day, Little Grey Rabbit was sad
without her tail but picked up her basket
and went into town. It was quiet in the
village and no one saw her slip through the
open door of the shop.

She gazed about at all the wonderful things, then spotted the picture of a carrot on a little packet. Quickly, she filled up her basket and fled for the door.

Little Grey Rabbit looked around anxiously, but saw no one except for five ducks. And as she walked she made plans for all the things she would grow in her garden.

When Little Grey Rabbit got home, no one was there, and the door stood wide open.

"Oh no," she cried. "Has the weasel got Squirrel and Hare?"

She took her scissors, a rope and a stick and went to look for her friends.

By the brook she found marks in the grass leading to an ugly black house. There she lay down under a bush and waited.

Before long, the door opened and the weasel stepped out.

And the moment the weasel looked away, Little Grey Rabbit dashed into the house.

"Hare, Squirrel, are you there?" called Grey Rabbit.

"We're here. Save us!" they cried from inside a bag.

Rabbit cut it open. "Take this rope and climb out of the window," she told them.

Then Little Grey Rabbit seized a stool and crept into the bag with it, just as weasel returned. "I'll roast them both," he said, and he brought his stick down hard on the bag – bang!

"Dead, both dead," he said. He didn't know that Hare and Squirrel had run away and Rabbit was safe beneath the stool!

As the weasel opened the oven door, Grey Rabbit slipped out, gave him a great push and shut him in the oven. Then off she ran, not stopping till she reached home.

"Oh Grey Rabbit," said Squirrel and Hare.
"We're sorry. We'll never be proud and vain again.
You saved us, and if that weasel comes back–"
   "He won't, he is roasted by now," she
interrupted, and told them all her adventures.

So they lived happily
together, and had a
fine crop of carrots.
And sometime I shall
tell you how Grey
Rabbit got her tail
back again…

THE END

A TEMPLAR BOOK

This edition first published in the UK in 2018 by Templar Publishing,
an imprint of Kings Road Publishing, part of the Bonnier Publishing Group,
The Plaza, 535 King's Road, London, SW10 0SZ
www.templarco.co.uk
www.bonnierpublishing.com

Original edition first published in the UK in 1929
by William Collins Sons & Co Ltd

This edition edited by Susan Dickinson and Ruth Symons
Additional design by Nathalie Eyraud and Adam Allori

3 5 7 9 10 8 6 4 2

ISBN 978-1-78741-226-2

Printed in China